Joy and smiles are in store for you!

Loretta Hayward

# On the Banks of Durbin Creek
# "Four Seasons for Bunnies"

Written & illustrated by
Loretta Hayward

Garden Gate Publishing

Published by Garden Gate Publishing
600 Griffin Rd.
Fountain Inn, SC 29644

Scripture quotations are from the Holy Bible, King James Version.

ISBN:978-0-9790884-1-4

**Library of Congress Catalog Card Number:**
Printed in the United States of America

Visit Garden Gate's exciting website at **www.gardengatecards.us**

# *Dedication*

*For my dearly beloved husband Glenn,*

*and my dearly loved children*

*Ronald, Benjamin, and Gloria.*

*My heart rejoices over the love and joy*

*that you bring into our lives together!*

Simple pleasures are life's greatest treasures.

"Don't be surprised if the smiles our cute bunnies bring
Cause you to laugh or make your heart sing!
This merry joy is such a wonderful thing.
Share it and spread it like sunshine in Spring!

# *Introduction*

Greetings from Garden Gate® Rabbit Park! We live on the banks of Durbin Creek! Our family raises all the adorable rabbits that you read about in our books! The hard work managing our rabbitry and gardens is not nearly as interesting as the visits with our bunnies and photo sessions when we dress the bunnies to take their pictures! (Some people have already requested that we write a book about that too!) There is a lot of excitement found on Durbin Creek that we love sharing with our readers! This is our second book where you will meet more of our sweet rabbits. Our photographs will allow you to see some of the differences in our rabbit breeds that make them so unique and also great illustrations. I enjoy drawing and photographing our rabbits as they grow up. They are very entertaining and delight us with their varied expressions that reflect their curiosity and pleasure- especially when they are loose in our flower bed or garden!

Our books are useful teaching tools and beneficial to many age groups for reading and writing skill development. The visual appeal will make lessons interesting and unforgettable! "Four Seasons for Bunnies" introduces the four beautiful seasons that we experience in South Carolina. Our seasons vary in temperatures and time according to the location in the United States, in the North American continent and also in the northern hemisphere of our earth. God created all things in a unique and wonderful way. The glossary on the last page is a very helpful tool. It defines our four seasons and several words used throughout this book.

Our rabbits remind us of the loveliness of creation and many precious memories we have shared with friends and families over the years! Gather the family together and celebrate the four seasons with us!

*~Loretta Hayward*

# Spring

In the spring time of the year
buds and blossoms reappear.
Baby bunnies will be born
in the early hours of morn.

*"For, lo, the winter is past, the rain is over and gone;*
*The flowers appear on the earth; the time of the singing of birds is come."*

—Song of Solomon 2: 11,12

Springtime
is for bunnies
newborn in their nest.
Amid morning dewdrops
peacefully they rest.

*Young Satin bunnies enjoy a beautiful spring morning.*

# Springtime is Seedtime

Springtime is seedtime,
Water and feed time.

*Choose healthy seeds to plant in rich soil.*
*Cover the seeds with dirt and water daily.*

## Springtime is sprout time

*Seeds germinate. Young new plants grow*
*from the seed. New shoots grow tiny*
*green leaves.*

## Springtime is weed time.

*Weed seeds in the soil will grow in your*
*garden. Pull up the wild weeds and allow*
*your sprouts to use the water and soil for*
*growth!*

O how thankful I can be with this feast set before me!
With great joy I truly pray, "You have blessed me Lord today!"

The strawberries
have finally ripened.
They are red
and so juicy-sweet!
Every bite is purest pleasure.
Every mouthful
a special treat!

*Mini Rex love strawberries too!*

# Summer

"He did good, and gave us rain from heaven, and fruitful seasons,
filling our hearts with food and gladness."

—*Acts 14:17*

It is summertime for bunnies. They are having so much fun.
Very early in the morning they are playing in the sun.

*Dutch family in the garden.*

## Our Fine Garden Feast

To the garden I must hurry
To the garden I must go
Early in the morning
I must visit every row.

With dewdrops on the lettuce,
So crisp and sweet they taste.
Early is our harvest—
No portion will we waste.

Let us picnic in the garden!
The finest feast is growing there.
Vine ripe bounty now awaits us—
A basket banquet we can share!

# Sunny Summertime

Miss Amelia loved the sunny summer days.
She hummed a happy tune and sorted the garden
vegetables that were picked that morning. The red
tomatoes looked so lovely. Two baskets were filled with
cucumbers and squashes. There were green, red, and
yellow bell peppers too.
Miss Amelia took a bite of a cucumber and sang,
"How sweet to eat a garden treat in the morn–ing!"
It was a beautiful day to sing and a lovely time to eat!

The garden was a busy place every morning during the summertime. Miss Amelia helped the family with the chores and cheerfully worked through the day.

*Mini Rex love the garden!*   13

Earlier that day, Miss Amelia picked fresh salad greens. She rinsed them in spring water for the family to eat at their next meal. Herbs were gathered, tied with twine, and then hung up to dry. Suddenly, she heard the scamper of tiny little feet.

Miss Amelia stopped working and listened. She clearly heard the sounds of chewing.
"Crunch!"
"Munch, munch,munch."
Then she heard the sounds of nibbling.
"Munch, munch, munch."

She knew the sounds of
"Nibblemouse!"
"That must be who it is! "
said Miss Amelia as she looked around the sacks and baskets. Then she saw Nibblemouse on the top of a burlap sack. Nibblemouse was boldly chewing on a new cucumber without an invitation.
"Oh dear, she has no manners at all!" Miss Amelia exclaimed.
"If she needed something to eat she should have asked politely."

15

Nibblemouse was a very greedy, untidy mouse. He leaped into the next basket and dug into the green beans. Then he made an awful mess as he pulled beans out of the basket and dropped them onto the ground. Nibblemouse rudely scratched the new tomatoes and knocked several into the dirt.

Miss Amelia had to stop Nibblemouse!
All the vegetables would be in ruins.

Miss Amelia waved her arms and yelled,
"Shoo! Shoo!"
"Thief!"

Nibblemouse scurried around Miss Amelia
knocking over more baskets.

Rabbits working in the orchard heard the shouting. They stopped picking peaches to see if Miss Amelia needed any help. They saw Miss Amelia waving a garden rake and chasing Nibblemouse around the vegetable stand. Some of the workers loved a good chase and ran with Miss Amelia after Nibblemouse. It was an exciting chase!

Nibblemouse finally escaped by hiding in a hole under the lilac bush.

All the garden rabbits were tired, hungry and ready for a rest.

Miss Amelia served everyone a delicious summer salad of fresh garden greens, sweet peas and carrots. They enjoyed the juicy plump peaches served for dessert. What a fine feast.

The family talked and laughed about how far they had chased Nibblemouse. They trailed that mouse through flower beds, the berry patch, and even the neighbor's chicken coop! Farmer Perkin's cat helped run the mouse past the beehives and into the next yard of lilac bushes.

Miss Amelia helped her family pick up the baskets and the mess that was made by Nibblemouse. She smiled and hummed a happy tune. Nibblemouse would not be back for a long, long time.

# Autumn

"While the earth remaineth, seedtime and harvest, and cold and heat, and summer and winter, and day and night shall not cease."

—Genesis 8:22

Our tan enjoys the autumn flowers!

## Autumn Harvest Time

God's garden gifts are growing
Through the spring and summer rain.
They are given during harvest
As we reap the golden grain.

While we gather all the fruit
Picking grape and pumpkin vine,
Our gifts are gathered daily
During autumn harvest time.

*This Netherland Dwarf has a full load.*

21

# The Giant Pumpkin

Have you heard about our pumpkin?

It is really big!
My brother Buckwheat says it is huge!
Mother thinks we have an enormous
pumpkin. (I like that "big" word too.)
Father said it is actually a giant pumpkin!

We have a big, huge, enormous, giant
pumpkin!

When Father planted the pumpkin patch
this summer, I did not know that pumpkins
could grow so tall.

It took two days to move that giant pumpkin
into the pole barn. The neighbors came over
to help. Father told us if we did not get it into
the pole barn then we would use it for a corn
crib or a henhouse!

Buckwheat and I made big plans. Whenever our work was done we went to see the giant pumpkin.

Buckwheat was the first to climb to the top of the giant pumpkin.

Buckwheat helped me climb the ladder for the first time!

I decided to leap just like Buckwheat!

I soared through the air and landed in the soft hay!
It was thrilling!
We had so much fun leaping off of the pumpkin into the air.
I was flying– just for a moment.

Landing on the haystack and rolling off was great fun!

Landing on my brother was fun too!

Over and over we climbed the ladder and jumped off the giant pumpkin.

Then we layed in the hay to rest.
We were too tired to move.
We could not even open our eye..z Z-Z-Z-Z-Z-Z-Z-Z

*New Zealand bunnies sleeping!*

# Winter

"*Thou hast set all the borders of the earth:
Thou hast made summer and winter.*"

—*Psalms 74:17*

In wintertime
the fallen leaves seem to disappear.
The colder temperatures
are often quite severe.
Rabbits now are wearing
their thick furry coats.
Some bunnies will be wrapping
scarves around their throats.

*A fun ride for Rex rabbits!*

# Snow Fun For Bunnies

Once upon a winter's morning the first snow began to fall. Silently, frosty white flakes drifted down from the heavens above.

Snowflakes gracefully swirled through the air and quietly laid a lovely white cover over the whole countryside. Every tree and field, every hill and hollow was wearing white. Snow covered the brambly woods and mossy bank beside Little Durbin Creek.

Every winding rabbit trail and home was covered with snow.

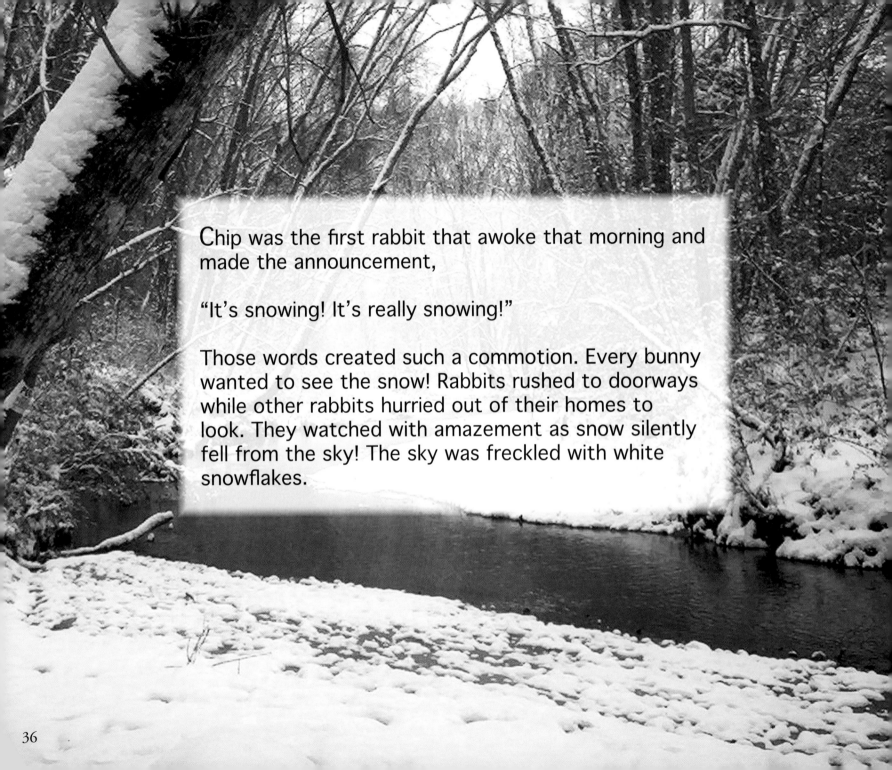

Chip was the first rabbit that awoke that morning and made the announcement,

"It's snowing! It's really snowing!"

Those words created such a commotion. Every bunny wanted to see the snow! Rabbits rushed to doorways while other rabbits hurried out of their homes to look. They watched with amazement as snow silently fell from the sky! The sky was freckled with white snowflakes.

Some rabbits got so excited that they scurried from their homes and leaped into the nearest snow bank.

This was a new and wonderful experience for the youngest bunnies. They were seeing snow for the first time in their life. The cold white flakes landed on their surprised faces and tickled their whiskers. Bunnies were digging and burrowing in the cold snow drifts until they were out of sight!

Chip and Lester joined all the fun. They loved the snow! They buried their nose into the snow and tasted the cool icy crystals. The snow was firm enough to shape and even packed into balls! Lester decided to make a giant snowball. As he rolled his snowball over the ground it grew bigger and bigger. Chip helped roll the large snowball. As the ball of snow got larger, it became heavier and harder to roll.

Soon the snowball was too big to roll.
What would they make with their giant snowball? Lester had an idea!
He rolled another snowball.

Chip helped
him lift it up onto the
larger snowball.
Whew! It was hard work!

They were making a
giant snowman!

They
packed more
snow around the
middle to hold it
all together.
Next,
they needed
to make the
snowman's
head.

43

"Will this do?" Chip asked,
He lifted another ball of snow up onto the top of the snow man.

Chip gave the snowman a hat and scarf while Lester made arms out of sticks.
Then they made the snowman a happy face. Buttons were used to make two round eyes.
The mouth was made from pieces of coal.

Chip gave the snowman
a lovely pointed nose.
It was a carrot from the
root cellar.

What a fine nose!

A sweet crisp carrot makes a fine nose.
Mmm, and a delicious nose. Chip
couldn't help but nibble a bit on the
end of the nose. The more he nibbled
the shorter and shorter the carrot nose
appeared to be.

"Oh my, this nibbling must stop before your nose disappears entirely!" Chip said.

"Forgive me dear friend."

When Chip looked at the snowman and saw his smiling face-he smiled back. What a fine fellow he is. Chip and Lester smiled at each other. They were both very pleased with their work and their new friend!

# Glossary

**Amazement-**a strong feeling of surprise

**Amid-**to be in the middle of

**Announcement-**message or public statement

**Autumn-**season between summer and winter. Time of harvest

**Banquet-**lavish meal of many courses

**Bee hive-**a structure housing a colony of bees

**Borders-**land lines that separate countries

**Bounty-**a plentiful supply

**Brambly-**area with prickly bushes

**Burlap-**a coarse cloth woven from jute

**Burrowed-**a small snug place created by digging

**Cease-**bring to an end

**Chase-**to quickly follow in order to catch

**Chores-**everyday jobs that are done regularly

**Commotion-**noisy confusion

**Coop-**an enclosure for chickens

**Crystals-**form of a snowflake

**Dessert-**a sweet course eaten at the end of a meal

**Dewdrops-**a drop of water condensed on a cool outdoor surface

**Enormous-**unusually large or great in size

**Entirely-**complete; in every sense

**Experience-**knowledge gained through being involved in something

**Fine Fellow-**better than average object

**Freckled-**to become marked with

**Fruitful-**highly productive

**Germinate-**start growing from seed

**Giant-**much larger than is usual

**Gracefully-**showing elegance and smoothness of movement.

**Greedy-**wanting or eating more than is needed

**Harvest-**crop that is gathered or ripens during a season

**Herbs-**plant used fresh or dried for seasoning

**Hollow-**low-lying area of ground

**Invitation-**encouragement to do something

**Lilac-**an ornamental bush that flowers

**Orchard-**land on which fruit or nut trees are grown

**Portion-**a part or section of a complete part

**Reap-**to gather or obtain something

**Reappear-**come back

**Rinsed-**to wash

**Root cellar-**underground room for storage

**Ruins-**something completely lost or destroyed

**Severe-**very harsh or strict

**Spring-**the season between winter and summer when plants bring forth leaves and flowers.

**Sprout-**to develop buds or shoots

**Summer-**warmest season of the year, falling between spring and autumn. Runs from June to August

**Swirled-**a turning, twisting, spiraling movement

**Thief-**somebody who steals something

**Trailed-**to follow an animal by staying close

**Tune-**song or short piece of music

**Twine-**string or cord

**Untidy-**to mess up something that was tidy or neat

**Vegetable-**a plant with edible parts

**Vine-**climbing plant

**Waste-**use something up carelessly,

**Whiskers-**short stiff hairs growing on a bunny's face

**Winding-**made up of many curves or twists

**Wintertime-**the season of the year between fall and spring, from late December to late March

**Wrapping-**material used to cover up